(60)

GRANDPARENTS
A Special Kind of Love

Eda LeShan

GRANDPARENTS
A Special Kind of Love

✖   Illustrated by Tricia Taggart   ✖

Macmillan Publishing Company
New York

Macmillan books are available at special discounts
for bulk purchases for sales promotions, premiums,
fund-raising, or educational use. Special editions
or book excerpts can also be created to specifica-
tion. For details, contact:

Special Sales Director
Macmillan Publishing Company
866 Third Avenue
New York, N.Y. 10022

Macmillan Publishing Company
866 Third Avenue, New York, N.Y. 10022
Collier Macmillan Canada, Inc.
Printed in the United States of America
10 9 8 7 6 5 4 3 2 1

Library of Congress Cataloging in Publication Data
LeShan, Eda J.
Grandparents: a special kind of love.
Summary: Explores the unique relationship between
grandchildren and grandparents, and discusses ways to
deal with conflicts and problems that may arise.
1. Grandparents—Juvenile literature.   2. Inter-
personal relations—Juvenile literature.   3. Love—
Juvenile literature.   4. Conflict of generations—
Juvenile literature.   [1. Grandparents.   2. Conflict of
generations]   I. Taggart, Tricia, ill.   II. Title.
HQ759.9.L47   1984   306.8'7   84-5673
ISBN 0-02-756380-4

For Rhiannon,
with a special kind of love

Contents

GRANDPARENTS
A Special Kind of Love

Introduction

I was a very lucky little girl. I had four grandparents who I knew loved me a lot. Even though I couldn't understand the language that my father's parents spoke, they smiled at me and hugged me. Whenever I went to visit those grandparents, they gave me little presents, usually a handkerchief or some candies. My grandmother cooked wonderful meals for me. We weren't able to talk to each other in English, but somehow I knew these grandparents were very glad that I'd been born.

I saw my mother's parents much more often. For a while I even lived in their house. My grandma let me help her make wonderful desserts in her kitchen—things like strudel and yeast cake and chocolate cream roll. Whenever I got sick, my grandmother would come to see me. She taught me lots of games like Old Maid and Casino and Hangman's Bluff and Tic-Tac-Toe, and told me wonderful stories about eveybody she knew. She never seemed to get tired of talking to me. She always brought me something delicious to eat, and somehow, no matter how sick I felt before she came, I'd feel much better as soon as I saw her. I remember her as the most *comfortable* person I ever knew.

My grandpa had a big dog named Grumpy. The three of us went for long walks together. Sometimes we would go to an ice cream parlor and my grandfather would buy ice cream cones for all of us. I'd hold Grumpy's cone while he licked the ice cream. When my grandfather came home from work, he always had a surprise for me in his pocket, and I would have to find out which pocket it was in. When he ate his soup, he made a funny noise, like "zzuuup," and that made me laugh. I used to watch him shave in the morning. In those days men had razors that they sharpened on a long leather strap and big mugs for shaving cream.

My grandfather had been married to another woman who was my mother's birth mother, and that woman had died. I was named after her, and I knew that my grandfather was very glad there was a new "Eda" for him to love. His second wife was the grandmother that I knew, and when I was very young, these two people always could make me feel safe and happy and loved.

Now I'm a very lucky woman because I have a

granddaughter. Whenever I see her, and she calls me "Grandma," I forget my worries, I forget the aches and pains I sometimes have now, I forget about *everything* except what a wonderful feeling it is to love a grandchild and have a grandchild love me. I can't think of anything more exciting than to watch her grow up.

But even though I have been so lucky, I know that grandparents and grandchildren sometimes can have a hard time understanding each other. I worried when my grandparents seemed angry or wanted to be alone or got tired. I thought it was my fault. I'm sure there will be times when my granddaughter will worry if I lose my temper or get too tired to play with her. I'm sure that I'll make her angry sometimes. I might even frighten her without meaning to do so.

I hope that she and I will be able to talk about feelings that bother us. I wish all grandchildren and grandparents could try to understand each other better and be able to talk to each other and figure things out. I was loved in a very special way by my grandparents and I love my granddaughter in a very special way— but even people who love each other may have a hard time understanding each other's feelings. I hope this book will help my granddaughter understand me, and that it will also help you to understand your grandparents better.

A Special Kind of Love

WHEN Larry goes to visit his grandfather, everybody tells him to be very quiet. "No jumping around or shouting," his father tells him. "Grandpa is very weak and tired."

Joyce doesn't see her mother's parents very often. They're always off somewhere playing tennis and golf.

Melinda loves to have Grandma come to visit. They hug each other and tell jokes and laugh a lot. Grandma always seems to understand how Melinda feels, even when her mother and father don't.

Jack's grandmother always wants him to show her his report card, and then she wants to teach him how to spell. When her friends come over to visit, she always wants him to play the piano. Jack has the feeling his grandmother just wants to be able to show him off, and it makes him mad.

GRANDPARENTS ARE HUMAN BEINGS

Grandparents come in all shapes and sizes; they're all different kinds of people—just like everybody else. They can be the best possible people you ever knew and they can also be people who make you feel very mixed up—even frightened or angry. They can make you happy and they can make you sad. Grandparents are full of surprises. You see Grandma on Tuesday and she teaches you a new game and a couple of funny songs she learned when she was a little girl in camp. Then you see her again on Saturday and she seems very sad and just wants to be left alone. Or one day Grandpa screams at you when you can't catch a ball and two weeks later he's quiet and patient and spends two hours teaching you how to play chess. What's going on here?

Nothing very surprising, after all. Grandparents are human beings just like all the rest of us. Parents can be plenty mysterious sometimes! And so can children. *You* don't feel the same way every day. Sometimes you feel friendly and sometimes you don't. There are days when certain things bother you. It's very hard to figure out what you or your mother or your father or your teacher will do on any particular day. It's hard to understand *anybody,* including ourselves—but it's very important to try to understand people because the more

· 7 ·

we understand ourselves and others, the better we feel.

Larry's grandfather has a heart condition and the people who love him are worried about him. Joyce's grandparents are a good deal younger and they pride themselves on having kept in good shape. For many years they both worked very hard in the hope that someday they could retire and play tennis and golf as much as they'd always wanted to.

Melinda's grandmother is a happy, busy woman. She grew up in a family where her mother and father (Melinda's great-grandparents) loved her a lot, and because she got a lot of loving, she has a lot of love to give Melinda.

Jack's grandmother, on the other hand, was always being criticized when she was a child. Nothing she ever did was good enough to suit her parents. She grew up feeling that she could never do anything right, so now she wants her grandson to be perfect. She doesn't realize she's doing the same thing to him that her parents did to her.

HAVING GOOD TIMES TOGETHER

Although there are surely times when a grandparent can upset you or make you angry or sad, most of the time grandparents and grandchildren can have a terrific time with each other.

Penny loves to hear how her grandma and grandpa arrived at the hospital just fifteen minutes after she was born, and how Grandma said that in her whole life she had never seen such a big, beautiful baby. When her grandparents come to visit, she loves getting out the picture albums and looking at all the pictures they took when she first walked alone and when she got a puppy and when she was learning to ride a bicycle. She loves the stories her grandfather tells her, stories that once, long ago, he used to tell her mother.

When Justin goes for a walk with his grandmother and she shows him all kinds of interesting bugs and leaves, his grandmother makes him feel like the most important person who ever lived.

Grandparents want to have fun with their grandchildren. They want to let their grandchildren know how important they are. Grandchildren are the future for grandparents. When a person has grandchildren, there is a wonderful feeling that a whole new generation is beginning and that the family will go on and on.

THE DIFFERENCE BETWEEN PARENTS AND GRANDPARENTS

One of the big differences between grandparents and parents is that usually parents worry about you more.

You are their child and they know how important it is to help you grow up into a strong, kind, responsible person. Very few parents feel sure, all the time, that they can do a wonderful job of helping you to grow up.

If, when you were much younger, you took a toy away from another child, your parents may have worried about whether or not they were teaching you about sharing and taking turns, and about private property. If you got very angry and hit another child, they worried about your temper, and how to help you tell people how you were feeling instead of hurting them. They worry about how well you will learn in school, and how you will find out what you want to be when you grow up. They want you to do the things you really want to do, but at the same time they hope you will be able to make friends and care about other people.

Being a parent is a very big job. It takes a lot of time and energy to raise children. Parents have to work hard to earn money and buy food and cook and clean the house and do the laundry. Sometimes they are too busy to pay attention when you want them to, or too tired to play with you, or it seems as if they are always warning or scolding or teaching you something.

Once upon a time, that's exactly what your grandparents were like when they were raising your parents. They weren't always sure they were good parents. They were probably quite relieved when your parents grew up, got jobs, got married and became parents themselves. When you were born, your grandparents most likely felt that now it was their turn to have a wonderful time with a child, without worrying so much. It wasn't going to be up to them to teach you everything you would need to know. All they would have to do is love you.

That's the special kind of love that can happen with grandparents. For grandchildren, it can mean having the warm and delightful feeling that your grandparents love you just because you were born and not because of anything else. They can love you just the way you are because they know your parents have the harder job of raising you. Most of the grown-ups you meet want you to do something or learn something or look a certain way. If you are very lucky, your grandparents are people who will think you are wonderful without your having to do anything to earn so much love.

UNDERSTANDING GRANDPARENTS ISN'T ALWAYS EASY

Sometimes grandparents can be confusing. Jay thinks it's terrific when his grandpa gives him a baseball mitt and a bat, but he gets angry when Grandpa tells him

over and over again that there's a better way to hold the bat. One day Richard's grandmother can play with him for hours and hours, and on another day she doesn't want to play at all. Sara can't understand why both sets of grandparents seem to love her and her brother a lot but often say bad things about each other. Her two grandmothers compete with each other; if one buys her a present, the other buys a better one right away. They all seem to want her to say which one she loves the best. It's nice getting presents, but it's not nice to feel she's supposed to choose favorites.

Even where there is a special kind of love, things can get very complicated. The more we understand our own feelings and the feelings of other people, the more we are able to enjoy all the wonderful parts of loving and being loved.

When Jay's father was a little boy, he just hated baseball and his father was very disappointed. When Jay shows an interest in baseball, Grandpa feels he has a new chance to have a baseball player in the family, and maybe he gets carried away. If Jay could say, "I like baseball, but I can't learn so fast," he might be able to slow Grandpa down a little.

Perhaps Richard's grandmother isn't feeling well and nobody wants to tell Richard about it because they don't want him to worry. It might be a good idea for Richard to ask his parents why Grandma seems to want to play a lot on some days and doesn't seem even to want him around at other times. He might tell his parents, "I'd much rather know what's the matter than always be so mixed up."

The reason that Sara's grandparents behave the way they do is that they are all worrying about being loved. In some way, they each feel unsure and need their grandchildren to give them more self-confidence.

This is what happened, long before Sara was born. Grandma and Grandpa Nelson never had much money and neither had gone to college. Grandma and Grandpa Mathews were very rich; they both had a good education. When Sara's mother and father said they wanted to get married, both sets of parents were against it. It seemed to them that Sara's mother and father came from very different backgrounds. Sara's four grandparents felt uneasy with each other. The Nelsons felt the Mathewses were looking down on them and the Mathewses felt the Nelsons were unfriendly.

The two sets of in-laws hardly ever saw each other and were just barely polite to each other until Sara and her brother were born. Then both families realized how very much they wanted grandchildren and how much they wanted their grandchildren to love them. They became rivals for their grandchildren's affections.

Once Sara and her brother know about the past,

they can not only understand their grandparents, but may even be able to help them. What they can do is let their grandparents know that they are glad to have four grandparents who are different from each other and that they love each grandparent for what makes him or her special and different from the others.

THAT SPECIAL LOVE

David and his parents and his brother and sister all live together in Grandma's house. One day when David came home from first grade, he told his grandmother that she had to go to school with him the next day. Grandma was a little puzzled about this. She asked David if he was sure the teacher hadn't said that his mother should come to school. David said he was sure, so the next morning Grandma went to school with him.

The teacher seemed a little surprised when she saw Grandma, and then she smiled. "I think I know why you brought your grandmother to school today, David, and I think it's very nice," she said. Then the teacher turned to David's grandmother and said, "I asked the children to bring one of their *favorite things* to school today. I guess I thought they would bring a favorite toy or a book—but I think it's lovely that David feels *you* are one of his favorite things."

That was one happy grandmother! David had let her know just how much he loved her and that his love for her was different from his love for his mother and father, or anyone else. If we are lucky, we learn when we are very young that grandparents can give us a very special kind of love—and that we can love them back in a very special way.

But grandparents are human beings with some of the same kinds of mixed-up feelings that you have sometimes. They have their own different personalities, imperfections, weaknesses and strengths, just like everybody else. And since they have lived a long time, their ideas about some things may be different from yours or your parents'.

The more we understand the people we love, the better time we can have with them. When we are able to see our grandparents as real people, it is easier for that special kind of love to happen. And that's what the rest of this book is all about.

When Grandparents Were Growing Up

WHEN I was a little girl, there were so few automobiles that nobody ever had trouble parking a car on any street in New York City. If my granddaughter wonders why I get a little crazy driving on a big highway, surrounded by gigantic trucks, that's probably the reason. If she doesn't understand why I hate crowds, and why I don't want to play video games and can't stand loud rock 'n' roll music, it's probably because so many things were different when I was a little girl.

Stamps were three cents each and mail was delivered twice a day; a hot dog was five cents and a hamburger was ten cents. There were so few people that nobody ever stood on line at the post office or at the bank. A ride on a subway was five cents and we had streetcars instead of buses, except for one bus that was a double-decker, and if you climbed up a flight of stairs, you could sit on the top. In the summertime, some of these buses were open on top, and that was a wonderful ride. Nobody was allowed to stand up on the bus. There was a conductor as well as a driver and he never let more people on the bus than could find a seat.

The streets were quiet; I never saw big crowds of people. An iceman came every other day with a big block of ice over his shoulder for our icebox because there were no refrigerators then. My family boiled dirty clothes in a big tub on the stove and then scrubbed them on something called a washboard, which was a piece of metal with ridges in it, in a wooden frame; there were no washing machines.

There was no television. There were no computers. Nobody I knew had ever flown on an airplane, and if you wanted to go to Europe you went by boat, unless you were Charles Lindbergh. I remember the parade when Lindbergh came home after flying to Paris. It seemed the biggest miracle that ever could happen. If anyone had told me men would go to the moon, I would have thought they were crazy. There were no frozen foods and no supermarkets and only two really tall buildings in New York: the Empire State Building and the Chrysler Building. If my granddaughter doesn't understand why I hate going downtown in New York because of all the hundreds of skyscrapers, that's probably why.

SO MANY CHANGES FOR YOUR GRANDPARENTS

The way things are in the world that you live in right now will always seem to you to be the way things ought to be. All your life you will be more comfortable with the things that were familiar to you during your childhood. When you are old enough to have children and grandchildren, you will probably think that the world they live in is pretty strange. You won't like a lot of the changes that have taken place.

That's how it is for your grandparents. There have been more important changes in the way people live and work and travel during your grandparents' lifetimes than in hundreds of years before they were born! It's very hard for people to get used to so many changes in such a short time. You will understand your grandparents much better if you ask them to tell you about how the world has changed and what life was like when they were children.

If you have a great-grandparent, he or she was probably alive when there were few telephones, when very few people had electricity, when there were no radios and the car had just been invented. Most people still traveled in horse-drawn carriages and wagons. Just think about how strange the world must seem to great-grandparents now! All the things that seem so natural and not at all unusual to you sometimes still seem surprising to them.

BRINGING UP CHILDREN

Very often older people feel that the way they were brought up was much better than the way children are brought up today. Susan's grandmother told her that when she was a child she never knew a single person who was divorced. Susan could hardly believe it, but then she began to understand why Grandma was so upset when Susan's parents got a divorce. When Jeff talked back to his father, his grandfather was furious. He said, "No young boy was allowed to be fresh to his father when *I* was young. Bad manners is what's wrong with the world today!" Jeff and his father know they love each other and they both express their feelings very freely, but Jeff can understand how his grandfather could be upset if, when he was a boy, he had to be polite and quiet all the time.

When most of your grandparents were young, they were not allowed to say that they were angry with their parents. Nobody ever told them it was all right to be jealous of a new baby brother or sister. People said, "Children should be seen and not heard." In many homes the parents talked to each other at the dinner table, but the children were supposed to be silent, unless they were asked a question.

Most children were dressed in clothes that they were supposed to keep clean all day. They didn't usually go to school until they were six or seven, and few parents tried to teach children to read or write before they went to school. There were many places where children could go off and play all by themselves, and nobody had to worry about their safety.

Children were usually not told what was happening if a father lost a job or if an aunt and an uncle were having bad fights with each other. Most parents did not talk to children about sex at all. Many of your grandparents would have had their mouths washed out with soap if they used any swear words or words having to do with going to the bathroom. When grandparents get angry with your parents for telling you about the people next door who are getting a divorce or a cousin who is dying of cancer, or for answering your questions about things like where babies come from, it is because their childhood experiences were so different.

Parents today are often much more honest with their children. Family life is usually more informal, more easygoing. Your grandparents probably feel a little uncomfortable, even embarrassed, when they hear people talk to each other so openly about subjects they were forbidden to talk about when they were young.

When your grandparents were young, they saw many of their relatives all the time. Probably their parents or grandparents had come to America from some other country, and when they got here, families tended to stay together. People didn't move as often or as far away as they do now. Nobody could pick up and fly thousands of miles, and there weren't so many big companies with offices all over the country. It's hard for your grandparents to get used to having relatives who live far away.

Ginny's grandmother cries when she comes to visit and cries when she leaves. Ginny couldn't really understand this until her grandmother told her, "When I was a little girl, I saw my grandparents and aunts and uncles every week at Sunday dinner. It felt so good to be together. Now I only get to see you twice a year and that makes me lonely and sad."

THINGS THAT WORRY GRANDPARENTS

Many grandparents have been very successful at keeping up with the times. By being curious and open-minded and by "staying loose," they have been able to keep a youthful point of view and can recognize that many things are better now. Chrissy's grandmother told her, "I think it was *terrible* that nobody explained menstruation to me. I was frightened half to death, and I think it's wonderful that you aren't as ignorant as I was." Roger's grandfather said, "I envy you, Roger. When I was young, we just imagined flying across the country, or seeing something on TV that is happening five thousand miles away, or space travel. I think it's so exciting that all those things seem natural to you!"

But some of the criticisms that grandparents have about things that happen today are not merely old-fashioned ideas; some things have changed in ways that can be quite upsetting. Amy lives alone with her mother. Her parents have been divorced for three years and Amy's mother has had four different boyfriends. She tells Amy about her dates and asks Amy's advice. She sometimes lets the newest boyfriend stay over-night.

Amy heard her grandmother say to her mother, "It's terrible the way you try to make a pal out of your daughter. She's only ten years old; she's still a child. She doesn't need to know everything about your life. She's your *daughter*, not someone to dump all your problems on. Daddy and I treated you like a child no matter what was going on in our lives. I think what you are doing is disgraceful." Amy thought about it and she decided that her grandmother might be right about a lot of things.

"THE GOOD OLD DAYS"

Many grandparents talk about "the good old days" when they were young. Of course, we all have memories about our childhood, but it is also natural to forget some of the things that were not so wonderful.

Most of your grandparents grew up in a time when people seemed to think that everything was going to get better and better. The First World War was over and grown-ups felt there would never be another war.

An idea that was likely to have been part of your grandparents' world was, "What you don't know can't hurt you." People didn't believe in talking about unpleasant things. Maybe they thought bad things would go away if they didn't think about them. When I was a little girl, none of my school books said anything about the terrible things that had happened to the Indians in this country. None ever mentioned race prejudice. Slavery would be mentioned in one sentence and then the book would tell about George Washington Carver. I didn't realize that black people couldn't go to many schools or live wherever they wanted or get jobs in stores and restaurants and businesses.

In my whole childhood, I never heard about anybody who smoked marijuana or took dangerous drugs like heroin. I was never told about people who drank too much, or people who lived together and even had babies when they weren't married. Children were kept innocent of anything that was considered bad by their parents.

Amy's mother may have told her too much, but too much secrecy can be a problem, too. Not understanding something can make you scared and worried. Not being able to tell grown-ups how you are feeling when you are angry or sad can make you very upset. The same thing is true about things that are going on in the world. If people don't face the truth about things that are unfair, or about serious problems like people being hungry or countries that want to fight, we won't be able to do anything about them. It's sometimes very hard to figure out what is too much secrecy and what is too much truth. Many grandparents feel there was too little truth when they were children and much too much now!

ASKING QUESTIONS

The best way to understand more about the time when your grandparents were growing up is to ask them questions. Jonathan got a tape recorder for his twelfth birthday, and one of the first things he did was to ask all four of his grandparents to tell him stories about when they were young. His grandparents were delighted. One of Jonathan's grandfathers said, "You save this tape for your children and grandchildren, Jonny, and with what you will add to it, you'll have a story that will cover about a hundred and fifty years!" It makes grandparents feel very good to know that they are leaving a family history behind for future generations.

You might ask your grandparents to tell you about the Great Depression that started in 1929. Did your grandparents see men selling apples in the street? Did they hear about the stock market crash? Ask them about the "Okies"—did they know people who lost their farms and traveled to California to work in the fruit orchards? Ask them if they remember when Franklin Roosevelt was elected. Did they and their parents feel better or worse? Ask them to tell you about the speech where Roosevelt said, "We have nothing to fear but fear itself." If you and your grandparents see riots on television and they say, "Things were better in our day," ask them about the unions and the strikes and the police in the 1930s.

Your grandparents probably would love to tell you about train trips or boat trips they took. Trains and boats were the two means of transportation most people used for going long distances. I remember taking an overnight boat up the Hudson River to Albany. Now I cay fly there in less than an hour—and it still seems surprising! Most grandparents wish there were more railroads still around. Did your grandfather wave to the train engineer when he was a child? Did he have a set of electric trains?

You might want to ask your grandparents why they get very worried if you have a high fever. When we were young, there were no antibiotics to help make us well. Most of us knew children who got polio, and that was very scary. People got sick and sometimes died from measles and scarlet fever and smallpox and diphtheria. When I was a little girl, there was little anyone could do when we were very sick except give us aspirin or cough medicine and keep us in bed. Parents got much more frightened when their children were sick than they do today.

When your grandparents were young, there was much less entertainment. There were fewer restaurants. People did go to the movies, but they stayed home most of the time. Grown-ups read stories and whole families played games. Sports were very, very different than they are today. Baseball and football were games people played just for fun; they weren't big businesses. If you enjoy sports, your grandfathers probably have some good stories about what it was like to play or watch a game forty or fifty years ago. I say "your grandfathers" because not too many of your grandmothers were allowed to play in team sports. It wasn't considered ladylike.

You might ask your grandmothers how they felt about being taught that their only real goal in life was to get married and have children. Women were not supposed to think about being doctors or lawyers or business executives. It was all right to be a nurse or a teacher, but usually that was considered a job that a woman would give up once she had a family.

Ask your grandparents about what it meant to be a boy or a girl fifty or more years ago. See if your grandfathers ever washed the dishes or cooked a meal or did the laundry. Ask your grandmothers if they ever took "shop" in school; ask your grandfathers if they ever took cooking or sewing. What you probably will find out is that they were raised to think that men and women each had separate jobs—and women didn't have very many choices.

Martha's grandmother started college when she was forty-five years old and now she's a lawyer. "I'm making up for lost time," she told Martha. "My father sent my three brothers to college but he wouldn't send me, because I was a girl. I'm glad I lived long enough to do what I always wanted to do."

Sam's grandfather, on the other hand, gets very angry at Sam's mother because she works in an office even though she has three children and her husband is able to support her. Sam heard his grandfather say, "They'll all grow up to be bums because you're not home to take care of them after school!" Sam asked his mother why Grandpa felt this way and his mother said, "Grandpa can't help it. That's what he was taught when he was young."

Some grandparents change; some find that too hard to do. By asking questions, you can begin to understand which grandparents feel comfortable with most of the changes that have taken place in their lifetime and which ones have a hard time. When you ask questions about that, you will find that there are no right or wrong answers for everyone. Peter asked his grandmother why she still stayed home and did all the cooking and cleaning and shopping now that women are supposed to be liberated. Grandma said, "I thought about it and I decided that I'm doing what I like best. I don't have to change just because other people aren't happy doing what I do."

Sometimes it's a good idea to ask questions at a time when grandparents seem most upset with you. Very often this happens when you forget to say "please" or "thank you," and a grandparent starts to give you a long lecture on politeness that begins with, "When I was a boy" or, "When I was a girl." That's a good time to ask how boys and girls were expected to act fifty years ago, and maybe your questions can lead to a most interesting discussion about how people treat other people. Together you might come to agree that it's harder to be polite today, when there are so many people and everything happens so fast, and there's so much noise and so many crowds—but you might also end up agreeing that even if it's hard, it's important for people to show they care about each other.

When your grandparents start yelling about how loud you play your records and how terrible the music is, ask them what *they* like. Jean's grandmother has records of all the Big Bands of the 1930s and the Broadway musicals of the 1940s and '50s, and Jean has discovered she likes them, too, although some songs are too slow and too sugary for her taste. Jean said, "Grandma, those songs are nice, but I'm going to play you some country music that doesn't sound too different. Just listen to the words."

By asking questions, you can start important conversations that help you and your grandparents understand each other's worlds—and when that happens, everybody gains.

Grandparents Are Still Parents, Too

ABBY'S mother was talking to *her* mother on the telephone. She began shouting, "I'm not a child anymore, and I wish you'd stop trying to tell me what to do!" Abby could understand how she felt. It's not easy having a mother boss you around, whether you are thirty-nine or eleven!

But it's not always easy for grandchildren to understand what's going on between their parents and grandparents. Ely explains it by saying, "I think of my mother and father as pretty old; they're old enough to take care of me and my sister. They're in charge of me. And then I hear my grandfather talk to my father as if he's a little boy! He tells my father to wear a sweater because it's cold outside! How could that be, when my father is a father and he tells *me* to wear a sweater?"

The reason this happens is because parents *never* stop being parents and children *never* stop being children, no matter how old they are. The memories of childhood are just too strong—they never go away altogether.

Cathy asked her mother, "Why is Grandma so happy when you ask her for a recipe? She acts as if you gave her a present!" Cathy's mother explained, "Well, Grandma's still my mother. She feels good when I do something that makes her feel as if I'm still her little girl, and I don't really mind. I know I'm a grown-up woman and a wife and a mother, and Grandma knows that, too, but once in a while she wants me to be her little girl again." Cathy asked, "You mean it's like when you want me to hug you and kiss you and sit on your lap even though I'm ten years old?" Cathy's mother laughed. "*Exactly* like that!" she said.

STRONG FEELINGS

Your parents and your grandparents have a history that you cannot share directly. They've known each other a very long time, and their relationship to each other is just as complicated as your relationship to your parents.

There are times when you feel that you are a disappointment to your parents. They seem angry or impatient and somehow you feel it's your fault. There are times when you get so angry at your parents that you even think about wanting them to go away and never come back—and then you get scared for even having such a thought. There are other times when you look at your mom and dad and suddenly feel a great big warm rush of love, and you think to yourself that you'll never be able to grow up and leave them—and that thought worries you, too.

When your mother feeds you chicken soup when you feel terrible, or your father surprises you with the new record you've been wanting, you think they are the most wonderful parents in the world. When your father says you can't stay up to watch a special television program, you think he's a big pain, and when your mother screams at you about leaving your bicycle in the driveway, you mutter a lot of words under your breath that you don't want her to hear.

Exactly the same kinds of things happened between your parents and your grandparents. They had good times and they had bad times together, but most of all they had very strong feelings about each other. Those feelings are hard to change, even when the children become grown-up people themselves.

ANOTHER CHANCE

It is impossible to be a perfect person or a perfect parent. Your grandparents may feel that if they could start over again, they would do a better job with their children, who are now your parents. But since their children are grown up, they feel it's much too late to try to change them. When a parent becomes a grandparent, he or she may think, *"Now* I have another chance! My children didn't grow up the way I expected them to, and I didn't always treat them the way I really wanted to, but maybe I can do a better job with my grandchildren."

Bruce's mother really lost her temper one day when his grandfather told Bruce he should go to summer school so he could get better grades in school. "Your grandfather is wrong," she said, "and it's none of his business. Daddy and I think you need a rest from studying, and that will help you do better in school." Bruce's grandfather couldn't understand why his daughter was so angry at him. He felt that he hadn't pushed his children hard enough and that it was his fault his daughter never went to college.

If grandparents couldn't afford to give expensive toys to their own children when they were small, that often made them sad. Marilyn's grandmother said, "When your mother was a little girl, she wanted a very fancy doll carriage for Christmas, and Grandpa and I had no money to buy it for her. She cried on Christmas morning when all we could get her was a small doll. I always felt so bad about that."

Marilyn's grandmother now has much more money, and she showers Marilyn with presents. Marilyn's father got into a serious argument with Grandma about this. He said, "I don't care how much money you have. Marilyn has to learn she can't have anything she wants the minute she wants it. I don't think children should have more toys than they can ever play with." Grandma felt very disappointed because for so many years she'd been waiting to be able to give presents to the children she loves.

Grandparents may feel that they were too strict when their own children were growing up. Just like your parents now, they wanted to do a good job of raising their children and they worried too much; they may feel they were too serious and didn't have enough fun with their children. Sometimes they want to make up for that with their grandchildren, and they try to have fun and be pals with them.

When Diane's grandmother took her to Disneyland, they had a wonderful time together. Diane couldn't get over how silly and giggly and funny her grandmother could be. But Diane is quite overweight, and she and her mother had been working together to try to help Diane lose some weight. On the trip to Disneyland, Grandma kept encouraging Diane to eat ice cream and hot dogs and jelly apples and popcorn and candy. She said, "It will be our little secret—we won't tell your mother."

The first and second time, Diane thought that was great, but after a while it began to upset her, partly because she was gaining more weight and partly because it felt funny not to tell her mother when she knew her mother was just trying to help her. Finally Diane said, "Grandma, if I were your daughter and not your granddaughter, would you want me to eat ice cream and not tell you?" Grandma looked very surprised and very thoughtful. "I'm sorry," she said. "I guess I just wanted you to have a good time with me." Diane hugged her grandmother and said, "I'm having a wonderful time—and we'll *both* tell Mommy that I have to diet when I get home!"

Noah's grandfather slipped him a dollar, secretly, every time he visited. He always said, "Don't tell your mom and dad." It made Noah feel funny. He couldn't figure out why this had to be a secret, and when he got his allowance each week, he felt guilty about not telling about having extra money. Finally he told his father, who thanked him for being so honest.

Then Noah's father said, "I'm very glad you told me, and now I never want you to tell Pop Pop that you told me! He wants to have that little secret with you—it makes him feel special. He thinks you'll love him more because he gives you money, and he likes to think that we are too strict and he's not. Sometime, if you feel like it, you could give him a big hug when he gives you the money and tell him you love him whether he gives you the dollar or not." Noah said, "Well, I think I'll tell him I love him, but it's okay if he wants to give me a dollar anyway!"

"When I visit my grandparents," Kerry says, "it's like Christmas all the time! We go shopping, and we go to movies and plays, and we play games, and we eat in restaurants almost every day, and I always come home with a suitcase full of presents. I'm so lucky to have grandparents who can laugh and sing and tell jokes and love to have adventures!" But Kerry knows that grandparents and parents are different, and she doesn't compare them to each other. She never asks her parents to be like her grandparents or to treat her the same way. That way, her parents don't get jealous or angry.

CAUGHT IN THE MIDDLE

Sometimes parents and grandparents seem to share a lot of unfinished business. They may have hurt each other or misunderstood each other, years and years before you were even born. There is no family where there aren't some serious arguments, and very often parents and children say things to each other that they may later regret.

Maybe your grandparents weren't very nice to your father when he first dated their daughter, your mother. Maybe your mother has never forgiven her mother, your grandmother, for not letting her go on a camping trip with her friends when she was a teenager. People change quite a lot by the time they get to be grandparents. Most of them become more patient, more understanding, than they were when they were raising children themselves. But your parents may still be angry at some of the things that happened when they were young.

John's father feels his parents loved their other son more than they loved him. Phyllis's mother has never gotten over the feeling that her parents didn't think she was pretty. When she hears her parents telling Phyllis how pretty she is, she feels a little jealous and angry.

Because parents and grandparents have had a whole life together that you were not a part of, things that happen between them may seem frightening and puzzling. You can't understand why they yell at each other—or, even worse, why they sometimes don't speak to each other. They may even complain about each

other to you, and that's the worst of all. Miriam's father says, "Your grandfather has the worst temper of anyone I ever knew." Miriam has never seen her grandfather yell. Frank's mother mutters under her breath as she's hanging up the phone, "I can't *stand* that woman another minute!" She's talking about his father's mother, and Frank doesn't understand why his mother hates her so much.

There may be times when grandparents say bad things about your parents—their very own children. They can be very critical. "Your father never stands up for himself—he lets everybody push him around." "Your mother certainly likes to spend money—it's a wonder you're not in the poorhouse."

Such talk can make grandchildren very unhappy. They don't like being caught in the middle between parents and grandparents; they don't like it if they are asked to take sides in an argument. Grandchildren need to let parents and grandparents know how they feel. Marty tells his father, "Maybe Grandpa wasn't such a wonderful father, but he's a good grandfather and I wish you wouldn't always keep telling me everything he did to you when you were a little boy."

THE GOOD PART

When we see parents and grandparents together, we

can learn quite a bit about our parents. We might begin to understand how a mother might have grown up with a lot of fears, if Grandma is very fearful, too. Or we might find out why Daddy boasts quite a bit, if his parents still act as if he isn't too smart. When Grandma talks so lovingly about Aunt Peggy, it's easy to see why Mom is jealous of her sister.

It may be a little frightening to think about our parents being children. We want them to be strong and wise, so they can take care of us. It's hard to see them treated like children by their parents. If it makes you uncomfortable, you can let your parents and grandparents know that children need both parents and grandparents *right now,* in the present.

Sometimes, though, it's comforting to learn that parents had some of the same problems you have now. Bob doesn't worry quite as much about being short when he hears that his father was the same way and then shot up suddenly when he was fifteen. Janice doesn't feel quite so dumb when she hears that her mother was terrible at arithmetic, too—and now keeps all the bank accounts. Anne doesn't feel so guilty about her mother's yelling at her, when Grandma says Anne's mother had a terrible temper even when she was a child.

Funny things can happen, too. One day Judy's grandmother called up Judy's mother and said, "Would you *believe* it? Momma just called me up to tell me to wear my boots because the weatherman predicted snow!" Judy's grandmother is fifty-nine years old, and *her* mother is eighty-one!

What you need to remember is that your parents are most certainly grown-up people, and they certainly can and do take care of you, but it's very hard for their parents to see them as grown-ups all the time. This is easy to understand if you think about how your parents treat *you*. Were *they* ready when you wanted to cross the street alone? Were *they* ready to let you pick out your own clothes when you went shopping? Don't they make you feel like a baby, sometimes? Because they have lived with you since you were born, they often have a very hard time realizing that you are growing and changing. Even when you may have children of your own, your parents will still tell you when to wear a sweater! And your children will have to learn just what you are learning right now—that nobody ever grows up completely in the eyes of a parent.

The Best of Times

THERE is one kind of feeling that helps a person grow up able to enjoy all the adventures of learning and loving, and that is knowing that you are wonderful and lovable just because you were born and not because of what you can do. It is being loved not because you can run faster than anyone else, or get the best marks in school, or have a lot of friends, but just because you are *you*. That is the special kind of love grandchildren need from their grandparents. When grandparents can give that kind of love, they and their grandchildren can have a special kind of fun together.

One four-year-old girl called her grandmother up on the phone one day and said, "Nana, I don't like it when you visit me and you have to go home, and I don't like it when I visit you and I have to go home, so I'm building you a tree house in our backyard!"

Many older children feel the same way about their grandparents. When they are having a lot of fun with each other, it seems to the grandchildren that it would be wonderful if they all lived together. Some grandparents *do* live with their grandchildren, and while they may still have many good times together, it is different from living apart.

LIVING TOGETHER

When people live together all the time, there are bound to be some difficulties. Just imagine what would happen if you only saw your parents once in a while; you'd be so glad to see each other—you would be overflowing with such loving feelings—that you would have the most fun you ever had. But when people live together all the time, it is impossible to avoid all the normal kinds of feelings people have sooner or later. People feel tired; people feel disappointed when things don't go well at school or at home or at the office. Parents and children feel angry and frustrated sometimes, and get annoyed with each other.

When Max yelled at his mother one day, and she told him to stop it, he said, "If I can't yell at *home*, where *can* I yell?" He had a good point! While we need to try hard to get along at home, the family is a safe place to let off steam once in a while because the people love each other enough to get over the difficult moments. Max can't yell at his teacher, and his father can't yell at his boss, and if Mom yells at the plumber, maybe he won't fix the sink. When people can't express their anger at strangers, they often express it at home.

When grandparents come to live with their children and grandchildren, they become part of the family. They, too, will feel impatient at times, or they may be too busy to play, or they may not feel well and want you to be quiet. No matter how much you love each other, living together usually means you and your grandparents are not going to get along well all of the time.

Kevin adored his grandmother until she had to come to live in his house after Grandpa died. Kevin had to give up his room and felt he had no privacy anymore. Grandma also worried about his going out with his friends, and she worried about his going ice skating on the lake, and she worried about his going alone on a bus. Kevin had never realized before that his grandmother was such a worrier.

In spite of these problems, Kevin's grandmother is still someone who has endless patience, who will play games almost all day when Kevin is sick and loves to take Kevin to plays and museums. They still have fun together—but not all the time.

When Brooke visits her grandmother, she knows that they will make up all kinds of games and stories and private jokes. She knows they will laugh a lot, that Grandma will let her stay up a little later and that she can play with Grandma's dog as much as she wants to. She knows that if somebody calls her grandmother on the phone, Grandma will say, "Can I call you back tomorrow? I'm entertaining my granddaughter today." It feels good to be the center of attention. But such visits are like going to a party. At home, Brooke can't play all the time. She has to go to school, help with family chores and take piano lessons. And Grandma says, "When Brooke goes home, I feel very tired. I have to rest for a day or two. I love our visits, but I'm glad we don't live together!"

Having fun with grandparents is a little harder when they live in the same house with you, but it still happens, especially when both grandparents and grandchildren think about planning special times together.

BOASTING

There is an old Spanish saying that if someone boasts a lot about himself, it must be because he has no grandmother! The idea is that if he had a grandmother, *she* would do all the boasting.

Sometimes it may be embarrassing or annoying to

have grandparents who always boast about how smart you are and about all the wonderful things you can do. But try just to sit back and enjoy it. Being boastful about grandchildren is another way in which grandparents show that special kind of love that makes you feel like a perfect person. Most grandparents are sure their grandchildren are the greatest children in the whole world.

Sometimes it gets very boring. Sometimes it can even make you feel worried and upset, because you don't see how any human being could possibly live up to this "dream child" your grandparents have created in their imagination. Probably the best thing to do is to let grandparents enjoy themselves, but also to realize they probably exaggerate quite a bit!

"What I like best," Bonnie says, "is that my grandparents always come to see me in every play at school, no matter how little my part is. And they clap the loudest and make a big fuss over me. Sometimes other kids in the play get jealous and they make fun of me, and I just say, 'You know how grandparents are,' but the truth is it makes me feel great."

ADVENTURES

It takes a long time for most people to learn that you can never accomplish anything at all unless you are willing to take risks—to try to do something you are not even sure you can do. When you are young, it seems very scary to raise your hand to answer a question in school because you might be wrong. Older people may be afraid to tell a boss when he or she is being unfair because they might lose their jobs. Sometimes people are afraid to go on a camping trip for the first time; they are afraid the tent might fall down or they might not be able to start a fire. Some children are afraid to learn to ride a bicycle because they might fall down, or they don't want to paint a picture because it might turn out to be a mess. Some people are afraid to say what they think because other people might think that what they said was dumb.

By the time a person gets old enough to be a grandparent, he or she usually has learned a very important lesson: You never can learn to do anything new, and you never can find out what you can do, unless you are willing to try, and unless you understand that people have to fail sometimes if they are ever to accomplish anything.

Grandparents who have learned this can be very adventurous. They might be ready to learn a new hobby—or even to take a trip down the rapids in the Grand Canyon. They can be silly without worrying about what people will think of them. They are willing to try new kinds of food or learn a new game, and they don't seem to care as much as younger grown-ups about how they look—if they are going for a canoe ride or to an amusement park, they want to be comfortable, and they don't care if people think they look funny.

But some grandparents are not adventurous at all. If their parents were very strict when they were young, or if they never got to feel really good about themselves, they may be afraid of trying new things, or of letting you try. They may worry too much about your safety, or be afraid you'll get sick if you try some new kind of food, or say, "Absolutely *not!*" when you want to go on a roller coaster.

In that case, it's a good idea to remember that adventures with grandparents don't have to be exciting to be fun. Maybe you can slowly introduce them to some little adventures, or you can find out what they did for fun when they were young. The best of times with grandparents are likely to happen when you begin to figure out what they are like, what makes them feel good and what makes them feel bad, what they enjoy doing and what they don't like to do at all. The real adventure is in learning about each other.

TIME ALONE

Especially when you have brothers and sisters, it's wonderful to have time alone with grandparents. Jimmy's grandfather loves to go fishing. Instead of taking all three of his grandsons on a fishing trip, he takes one at a time. At home Jimmy's younger brother follows him around all the time and bothers him a lot. His older brother is always telling him how to do something. But when Jimmy is alone with his grandfather, there is nobody to bother him or tell him what to do. "I'd rather go fishing alone with Poppy once a summer than three times with Paul and Lewis," he says.

Being alone with a grandparent can be a very special time. You don't really have to be doing much of anything. You can just be playing a game of checkers or learning how to knit or looking at picture albums. What seems to be very special is being able to talk to a grown-up who is *really* listening to you.

Niki's grandparents have ten grandchildren from the families of their three children. When each grandchild reaches the age of ten, a special trip is planned to some place that child wants to visit. It might be Disneyland or a boat trip down the Mississippi or visiting the Grand Canyon or taking a train across Canada. Niki's grandparents are fortunate in that they have enough money for these wonderful trips, but other kinds of trips can be just as wonderful when you have your grandparents all to yourself. Going out for a pizza, or going to a museum of science, a Wild West show, a zoo or an aquarium can all be very special times.

There are times when it can be more fun to have brothers and sisters come along. Grandparents can be too fussy or get too tired, and then it helps to have other children to play with. But once in a while, most children would like a chance to have a special private time with a grandparent. When you think you would like that very much, you might even suggest it.

Terry told her grandmother, "I like Benjy all right, but it's hard being around a baby all the time. Couldn't you and I have a special date sometime and leave him home with Mom and Dad?" They made a date to go shopping for some clothes for Terry to wear to school. While they ate lunch at McDonald's, they talked about a girl at school who was a bully. Grandma told Terry what she had done about the same kind of problem when she was a girl; she'd invited the bully in her class to come on a picnic with her family, and they'd ended up being friends. Terry felt so much better that on the way home she said, "Grandma, could we buy a present for Benjy?"

LEARNING SPECIAL THINGS

Grandparents often seem to have more time than parents to teach you special things that nobody else thinks are important. Jody's grandpa has a million "Knock Knock" jokes that he learned when he was in high school, and Jody loves to hear them. She and Grandpa make up new ones and laugh so hard it hurts. Vincent's grandfather is teaching him how to make fishing flies; it takes a lot of patience and delicate work, but Vincent's grandfather never seems to get tired of these lessons.

Very often grandparents feel that there are things they never had time to do with their own children when they were young that they can now do with their grandchildren. Elyse's grandparents told her that all their lives they'd wanted to learn how to sail a boat. They took her along when they went for lessons and then they bought a small sailboat. Elyse's grandfather said, "I'm the captain now, but someday you'll be the captain." Elyse was so happy and so excited that she told her mother, "I'm never, ever going to leave Chicago and Lake Michigan!"

Sometimes a grandparent may sing crazy, silly songs he or she learned at camp, or teach you soap carving or weaving. Mitchell's fourth-grade class is studying about Greece long, long ago. His grandfather once took a walking tour through Greece and knows all about the gods and the temples and the way the houses looked and the people dressed. When Mitchell brought some of his grandfather's pictures to school, his teacher suggested that he ask his grandfather to come and tell the class about his trip to Greece.

Some of the very best times grandchildren and grandparents can have together is when they teach *each other* things. There are so many things you are learning, so many things you are interested in, that your grandparents don't know anything about. You probably know much more about computers and space travel and many other things than your grandparents do. The most fun of all is sharing the things that interest each of you, asking questions about things your grandparents know, and telling about the things you know.

ALWAYS AND FOREVER

All kinds of things can happen to children. Many children have parents who have gotten a divorce; many other children worry about that happening. When parents fall out of love with each other, many children worry that their parents might fall out of love with them, too. Sometimes families have to move a lot, sometimes a parent or a brother or sister can get very sick, sometimes a parent may lose a job. There are lots of things that can make you feel worried and frightened. But one comforting thought is that no matter what happens, grandparents will still be your grandparents and will always love you.

After Bernie's parents got divorced, Bernie was very

sad and very frightened. He was also angry at his parents. He went to see his father's father and said, "Tell me some of your boyhood stories." He knew he would feel better if Grandpa reminded him of things that had happened to him long, long ago, on a farm in Nebraska. The stories were kind of quiet and simple—about milking a cow or chopping wood or walking three miles to school. Grandpa had lived with his six brothers and sisters, his mother and father, two aunts and a grandmother. Grandpa's stories made Bernie feel safe, somehow; they reminded Bernie that he was part of a big family with a long history and that many people loved him.

Grandparents can surely give you good feelings about yourself, and they can make you feel safe and add fun and excitement to your life—but that isn't always the way things are with grandparents. What you are learning as you grow up is that nobody is all good or all bad and that no experiences in life are all black or all white. Sometimes things are not so wonderful with grandparents, and we need to think about those times, too.

When Things
Are Not So Wonderful

AS you grow up, you will be learning that people who love each other can also hurt each other, and nobody is perfect; nobody even comes close. Even in the happiest families there are problems because people's feelings are so complicated. Chances are that even if you have some wonderful experiences with all your grandparents, there are times when things are not so wonderful. Grandparents and grandchildren can get angry and impatient with each other. It's more than likely that grandparents will sometimes do things that upset you—and that you will do things that upset them.

Some problems aren't too serious, even though they can be annoying. Allan gets furious when his grandmother treats him like a baby and fusses over him. Meg has a grandfather who is always telling her how to behave and is very strict in his rules. Ronny's grandmother is often very nervous and irritable, and he wishes he could go out and play and not have to try to talk to her and calm her down. Sometimes grandparents get too nosy—they ask you questions you don't want to answer.

Joanne's mother told her that her grandparents were coming to visit. Joanne said, "Oh, no! Now they are going to drive me crazy taking pictures of me every minute!" Leo's grandparents make a big fuss about his being polite, and they have a fit if he says a swear word that his parents don't seem to mind. Every person we ever meet has little quirks or opinions and attitudes that may be different from our own, but we learn to be tolerant of such things when we also feel a lot of love for the person.

MIXED FEELINGS

Some problems are more important and more serious. Alice feels very bad because one of her grandmothers seems to love her older sister, Marian, more than she loves her. Grandma always wants Marian to visit her but doesn't seem the least bit enthusiastic about Alice's coming along. Grandma criticizes Alice all the time: Her dress is dirty, her hair needs to be cut, her voice is too loud, she's not as smart as Marian was at her age. At the same time, Grandma is always raving about how pretty and polite and sweet Marian is.

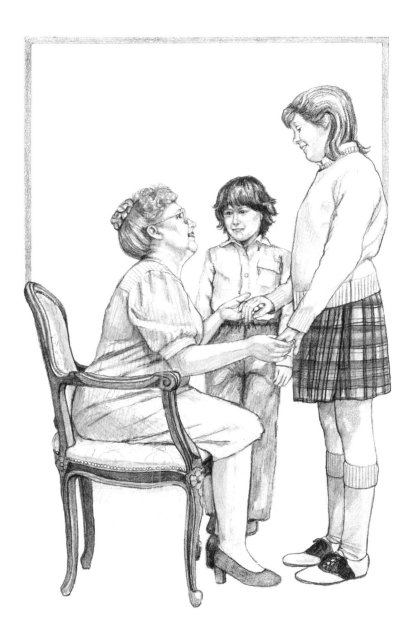

One day, after her grandparents had been visiting for two weeks, Alice's mother said, "I know it's very hard on you when Grandma's here because she shows such favoritism toward Marian. Grandma treated me the same way when I was a child, so I know just how you feel. Grandma prefers people who make a big fuss over her and behave just the way she wants them to. You and I upset her because we have our own ideas and we don't like other people telling us what to do. You and Marian will always have different friends. Some people will like her better; some people will like you better. Your other grandmother thinks you're wonderful!"

It's very hard to realize that neither parents nor grandparents ever treat any two children the same way. It often seems as if they are playing favorites or that they are being unfair. It will probably help in such situations to remember that *you* don't love anybody in exactly the same way you love somebody else. This is actually quite a wonderful thing, for it helps us to realize that every single person is different from every other person—and that makes life much more interesting. Some people hit it off right away; somehow their personalities just appeal to each other. Some people rub each other the wrong way, no matter how they may try to get along. It is important for Alice to understand that she is just as good as Marian, only different—and if she sometimes makes one grandparent feel unfriendly or uncomfortable, that doesn't mean there is anything wrong with her. The worst thing she could do would be to try to be exactly like Marian. Probably the best thing she can do is to try to get along with that grandmother and to accept the fact that while they love each other in some ways, they won't always get along too well.

It is easier to be sensible about mixed feelings when grandparents visit your home. It gets more complicated when you visit your grandparents in their home.

VISITS

Some visits to grandparents are wonderful, especially if they include a trip to Disneyland or a camping trip, or visiting New York and going to the Museum of Natural History. When your grandparents make plans for doing things you really enjoy, a visit can be like having a birthday party every day!

But even though you may love your grandparents and feel safe with them, you may still feel quite homesick. Sometimes grandparents fuss a lot and worry a lot. They treat you as if you were still a baby. Sometimes they want to show off to their friends and you get pretty bored with *that*! Sometimes frightening things can even happen.

While his parents took a trip to Europe one summer, Kenneth stayed with his father's parents. Things seemed to be going all right, but after a few days, Kenneth began to have terrible headaches. When he told his grandmother, she took him to a doctor to find out what was wrong. The doctor took Kenneth into his office alone, and they talked for quite some time.

Dr. Morgan told Kenneth, "I guess that maybe you're just a little angry at your parents for not taking you along on their trip. And on top of that, it sounds to me as if your grandparents make you a little nervous because they have such different ideas about some things. I'm going to give you some medicine for your headache, but what is even more important is for us to figure out some ways for you to feel less upset. Maybe you just need to tell yourself that it's okay not to love every minute of this visit and to feel a little angry at your parents for wanting to have a vacation without you. Your grandparents love you a lot, and they really want you to enjoy yourself. They tell me about you every time I see them. If you could get yourself to feel sort of like a rag doll—loosen up a bit and take things as they come while you get to know these people who care so much about you—you might even have a pretty good time."

Not every child is lucky enough to meet such a wise and sensible doctor while visiting grandparents! But his advice can be useful to you, if you get nervous or self-conscious or uncomfortable for some part of a visit. You might even pretend that you are on a special adventure, like a safari, where you are going to meet people you've never met before. You are going to try to learn as much about them as you can: how they think, what they feel, what happened to them when they were children, what trips they've taken, what famous people they know about who died before you were born, like Babe Ruth or Helen Keller. Find out about the things they remember and why they are Democrats or Republicans. These interesting "strangers" also happen to know just about *everything* about a certain grown-up who happens to be your mother or father, and if you play your cards right they could reveal some terrific stories!

There are some things about grandparents that you may not know until you visit them. Wendy, when she was five years old and visiting her grandparents, got up one night to go to the bathroom. She was half asleep, and when she turned on the bathroom light the first thing she saw was a set of teeth in a glass. She thought she was having a nightmare and shrieked in terror. She'd never seen false teeth before. Her grandmother came running into the bathroom and told Wendy she was being silly, but Wendy never forgot how frightened she was. Grandparents—just like many other adults—don't always understand the things children are afraid of.

Sometimes grandparents seem to treat you as if you were much younger than you really are. They think they have to watch you all the time; they don't realize how much more freedom and responsibility you now have at home. Maybe they haven't seen you for a long time and don't realize how much you have changed. You probably will have to do just exactly what you did at home to earn being treated as a more grown-up person—prove you're ready! It may take a few days, but *acting* more grown-up will get the message across far better than *telling*.

Jessica tried explaining to her grandmother that at home she was allowed to go to the supermarket on her bicycle alone. But her grandmother wouldn't let her go alone to a playground a block away from her apartment. On the second day of her visit, Jessica said she'd like to make breakfast for her grandparents. She knew exactly what to do. She not only made scrambled eggs and coffee, but she set the table and later washed the dishes. Her grandmother said, "You really *are* different and older! I'm very impressed!" Actions spoke louder than words.

One problem that often comes up in visiting grandparents is that you and they feel you have to be together all the time. This can be a great strain, for both children and grown-ups usually need some time alone. It's a good idea to take some books along for your visit and to tell your grandparents that sometimes you get tired and need to be by yourself for a while. They will probably look very relieved!

Joshua and his sister Gerry are eight and ten years old, and when they go to visit their grandparents in Florida, they have a hard time remembering not to run in the halls or laugh too loud when they go to the pool, and not to yell at each other when they are playing Monopoly. After the first Christmas visit, they weren't too sure they ever wanted to go again. When Grandma complained to their parents that they were disturbing other people, their mother said, "Well, maybe it would be better if you visited us for the next few years, until Josh and Gerry are older." Neither the children nor the grandparents liked that idea at all, because some of the time they had had a lot of fun. So Grandpa wrote a letter to Josh and Gerry. It said, "I have a very good idea. When you come to visit us, I'm going to take you to a playground near a school every morning and you can make as much noise there as you could possibly want to. Then it won't be so hard to quiet down in our house."

WHEN PARENTS AND GRANDPARENTS DISAGREE

Tommy knows his Aunt Felice is dying of cancer, but Grandma says, "Aunt Felice just has a stomach ulcer and she'll soon be well again." Lucy knows her grandfather has a very small pension, but he brings her expensive presents and says, "I'm really lucky that I have plenty of money to spend on the people I love." It can be uncomfortable and confusing if parents try to tell the truth about things that are happening and grandparents can't be quite as honest.

You need to remember that when your grandparents were growing up, they may have been taught that there are some subjects (such as money and illness) that nice people don't talk about. Your parents, on the other hand, probably grew up at a time when people were realizing that communicating honestly can be very important, no matter what the subject.

Even though parents and grandparents may behave differently about telling the whole truth, they probably have the same reasons for what they are doing. Most parents feel that honest answers can free you from confusion and fear of the unknown and can help you to trust them. They tell you the truth because they love you. Many grandparents were brought up to believe that children should be protected from painful facts. They don't tell you the truth because they love you. Love is the secret ingredient.

The most important people in your life right now are your parents. It's possible that when you grow up you will disagree with some of their ideas. But right now, if your parents and grandparents tell you different things, you need to pay more attention to your parents—unless something very, very bad is happening and you feel you really can't depend on your parents to help you.

Suppose, for example, a child's parents are separated and he lives with his mother, who is very sad and cries all the time and even forgets to buy food. If his father can't be reached, it may be important to write or call grandparents and ask for help. There are some parents who are too mixed up in their feelings to take care of their children—even some parents who get so angry they hurt their children. When such really bad things happen, it is time to ask for help, and grandparents are often the people a child can turn to.

But most of the time, what a grandchild has to do is listen with interest to grandparents' ideas—and maybe even behave differently while visiting them— but at home, until you are grown up enough to make up your own mind about important questions, you need to pay attention to your parents.

Gail's parents believe that the only reason a person

should work hard in school is because he or she wants to learn. Gail's grandfather tells Gail he will give her five dollars for every A that she gets in fifth grade. Gail would love to have extra money, but she also knows her parents feel very strongly about bribes. Her father says, "I'll talk to Grandpa and tell him that if he wants to help you celebrate when you get good marks, he can take you to a movie and treat you to a soda afterward. That way you can feel happy *together*." Gail feels relieved not to have to be caught in the middle.

When Sybil visits her grandparents, they expect her to kneel and say a prayer before she goes to bed. Her parents don't do that.

When Mary Ellen visits her grandmother, she gets all kinds of things to eat that her mother doesn't approve of—like cake and candy and ice cream. Her mother studies nutrition and knows a lot about health foods; Grandma says, "That's all a lot of nonsense."

What we all learn as we grow up is that each person has his or her own ideas and that it's not at all easy to figure out who is right and who is wrong. The more different ideas we hear, the better able we will be to make up our own minds when we grow up.

Marvin's grandparents are Jewish and they keep a kosher home, which means they follow certain rules about eating and saying prayers and observing special holidays. Marvin's mother was born a Catholic, but she and Marvin's father have their own personal religious beliefs and they don't go to a church or a temple. When Marvin was very young, he used to think that since his parents didn't do these things, his grandparents were a little peculiar. As he got older, he realized that his grandparents and his parents really believe in many of the same things. They want people to try to be good to each other, and they want a peaceful world. They just express these ideas in different ways. He has learned to respect his grandparents and he has even begun to enjoy visiting on holidays.

Respecting people who have different ideas is not at all the same thing as taking sides. Sometimes children have to remind their parents and grandparents that they don't want to take sides. Sal's grandfather is a Republican and he's always telling Sal how terrible the Democrats are. That makes his father, who is a Democrat, very angry, and so he gives Sal long lectures on why his grandfather "doesn't know what he's talking about." Each one wants Sal to agree with him. One day Sal told his grandfather, "When I'm old enough to vote, I'll make up my own mind, and I don't like it when you and Daddy say bad things about each other." Often children can help grown-ups to remember that people can have different ideas but still care about each other very much.

Some Different Situations

NOT only are all grandparents different, but children can have many different kinds of relationships with grandparents. Grandparents can be part of your every-day life or complete strangers. Some children see their grandparents almost every day. Many have grandparents living with them and their parents; a few are being raised by grandparents alone. Some children almost never see their grandparents. These different experiences help to influence how a child feels about his or her grandparents.

WHEN GRANDPARENTS LIVE WITH YOU

There can be both advantages and disadvantages to having a grandparent living in your home. If Mom and Dad both work, it can be comforting to know Grandma will be there when you get home from school. If you have to share a bedroom with a grandparent, you can feel angry about not having any privacy. Sometimes a grandparent will stick up for you when your parents get angry, but at other times a grandparent can pick on you and nag too much about what "nice children" do or don't do. If your parents and grandparents argue a lot, that may be very upsetting. You may also feel that having a grandparent live in your house takes away from your time alone with your parents.

It's easy to enjoy the good parts: having someone who is not tired play cards with you at night, or having a terrific cook around who makes wonderful pot roast and chocolate cake, or knowing that when Grandma tells a neighbor you are "the light of her life," she really means it. These are all extremely pleasant.

The problem is what to do about the not-so-wonderful things that can happen when a grandparent lives with you. One thing that won't help at all is to feel guilty because sometimes you get impatient and angry and wish he or she would go away. Those are normal feelings; they don't make you a bad person.

If you keep all those feelings to yourself, you will feel upset most of the time. All of us need someone to whom we can tell our troubles. Sometimes this can be a parent. Sally's mom whispered to her, one Saturday morning, "You and I are getting out of this house today! We're going shopping, and we're going to a Chinese restaurant for lunch, and *nobody* is going to try to boss us around!" Sally knew her mother meant Grandma. She also understood that her mother didn't mean they didn't love Grandma, only that Grandma got on their nerves sometimes.

Tim went to the school guidance counselor because he was getting headaches almost every afternoon. Mr. Kraft helped him to understand and express his anger at the fact that his grandmother had come to live with the family, and sometimes she treated him like a two-year-old. After Tim was able to talk about his feelings, he and Mr. Kraft figured out ways in which Tim could make it clear to his grandmother that he wasn't a baby, without hurting her feelings.

Sometimes a favorite uncle can listen sympathetically to your troubles, or maybe the mother of a friend. Sometimes brothers and sisters can have a "gripe session" that clears the air. Since good times as well as difficult times happen when a grandparent shares your home, it might help to remember that some grandchildren would give a lot to see a grandparent even once in a while.

WHEN GRANDPARENTS ARE STRANGERS

Some grandparents can become strangers over a period of years and then suddenly reappear into their grandchildren's lives. Miho and her parents were waiting at the bus station for her grandparents to arrive. They lived three thousand miles away and Miho hadn't seen them for four years. When they got off the bus, her grandparents expected her to hug and kiss them, but Miho felt very shy with them. She was quiet on the way home in the car. Her grandmother kept looking at her with hurt eyes, and that just made Miho feel worse. When they got back home, Miho's father whispered, "Just remember: They used to diaper me when I was a baby!" That made Miho laugh. Suddenly, she didn't feel so shy or strange, just thinking about the fact that her father had known these people every day since he was born.

If a grandparent whom you don't really know very well feels upset because you are shy, it might be a good idea to say, "Grandma, I haven't seen you for a long time and it takes me a little while to stop feeling shy." Saying it can make you feel better and also can help make grandparents feel more comfortable.

WHEN GRANDPARENTS DISAPPEAR

There are a great many children who never see one or more of their grandparents. This can happen for many reasons.

Jason's father died when he was five years old. It is now five years later and his mother is trying very hard to make a new life for herself and her son in a different part of the country. The grandparents who lost their son cried so much whenever they saw Jason that finally Jason's mother moved as far away from them as she could. She could understand their grief, but she felt that she and Jason would never be able to recover from their own sorrow if they had to go through so many tearful scenes every time they saw the grandparents.

Alison's father is a very unhappy person, sick in his feelings. He has a violent temper and Alison is scared of him, even though she loves him and feels sorry for him. One day when he really hurt her mother, Alison's mother decided they would have to leave. She took Alison and went to a shelter for wives and children who have been physically hurt. Alison's mother blames her husband's parents for his problems and never wants to see them again. Alison understands how her mother feels, but she also feels sad about losing half of her family.

Not all grandparents are loving and kind. The reason Kate and her brother, Edward, never see their father's parents is that their father doesn't want them to be hurt the way he was when he was a little boy. His parents are both alcoholics. They become very angry and strange when they are drunk. Edward and Kate's father left home when he was sixteen, and he doesn't want to have anything to do with his parents.

There are a few people who don't really want to be grandparents; it makes them feel old, or they don't want to feel tied down to anyone, or children make them nervous. So they hardly ever see their grandchildren. If this happens to you, just remember that it has nothing at all to do with whether or not you are a lovable person. It is very sad when someone can't give love, but while we can feel sorry for such a person, we must remember it is not our fault.

Sometimes parents may say, "Let's just not think about it," if there is a reason why one or more grandparents are not part of a child's life. The trouble with that is that being told not to think about something usually makes you think about it even more. Probably a better idea is to let your feelings of sadness or anger or curiosity or confusion come right out in the open. It is natural to have mixed-up feelings when there is any kind of problem in a family. The more you can feel your feelings and think about your thoughts, the more you will be able to go on growing and changing, learning and loving.

Jill is eleven years old and she doesn't remember her mother's parents at all. For that matter, she can't even remember her mother. Sometimes she wonders why all these people left her and she feels so sad she can hardly stand it. When she was about three years old, her mother had a mental breakdown—which means she got so sick in her feelings that she had to go to a hospital. Her mother was so upset that she could hardly talk to anyone and so sad she cried most of the time. At the hospital they did everything they could to try to help her feel better, but her doctors told her that she would never be well enough to go back to being a wife and a mother. Jill's mother got a divorce from Jill's father and went to live all by herself in another city. Jill's father was afraid that Jill might suffer too much if she saw how mixed up and sick in her feelings her mother was, so he insisted that Jill's mother was never to see Jill again.

Jill was too young when all this happened to understand it. Because she was only three years old, and this is the way young children think, she felt sure she had done something terrible to make her mother leave her. She was sure everything was her fault. She never asked her father any questions because she was too afraid. As she got older, she began to wonder about what had happened to her mother's parents. Nobody ever talked about them, either, but Jill could remember seeing a picture of herself with a tall, pretty lady with gray hair. She wondered why her grandparents didn't come to see her. Were they angry at her for making her mother sick?

Like most children who aren't told the facts, Jill

was very confused. What she didn't understand was that her mother had been an unhappy child, with many problems, long before she grew up and got married. Jill had nothing to do with her mother's being sick. The reason why her mother agreed never to see her again was that she thought Jill would have a happier life without her. Jill's father blamed her grandparents for what had happened to her mother. After the divorce, he moved far away and never let them find out where he and Jill were living. Jill's grandparents had tried very hard to find Jill, but they knew that even if they did, her father would do everything possible to keep them from seeing her.

Grown-ups sometimes make big mistakes about what will be best for a child. They feel that they are showing love for a child and protecting a child when they are really doing the opposite. Once in a while, lying in bed at night, Jill thinks maybe she'll try to find her mother and her grandparents someday, when she's older, but then she thinks that might hurt even more, because they don't seem to care about her. Meanwhile, her grandparents think about her and miss her, every single day.

Charlie's parents are divorced. They live three thousand miles apart. Charlie lives with his mother and his stepfather and his stepsister. He visits his father during school vacations. He sees his mother's parents about twice a year, but he never sees his father's parents. He doesn't talk about it, but deep inside he misses them almost as much as he misses his father. His stepfather, Harry, has parents who live nearby and he sees them all the time. Somehow Charlie feels guilty because he likes them so much! He feels as if he's being disloyal to his father and the grandparents that he never sees.

One day his stepgrandfather took him fishing. After their picnic lunch, he told Charlie, "I know you miss your father and his parents. It's very hard for a kid to get over a divorce and a parent's remarriage. I just want you to know that Grandma and I are really crazy about you, and if you feel sad sometimes and want to talk to us about it, that's okay." Charlie felt so full of love for this new grandparent that he couldn't say anything. But he didn't feel so guilty anymore.

As we grow up we learn that life can get very complicated and we can feel worried and unhappy quite often, but there are almost always some good things that can happen if we let them. It wouldn't help Charlie's father or his grandparents if Charlie had no grandparents to love. He decided it was pretty lucky that Harry's parents made him feel so good.

Sometimes, of course, children lose touch with grandparents just because they live too far apart and can't afford to travel to see each other. All four of Bill's grandparents live in New York, and he and his sister and his parents all live in Oregon. Bill talks to his grandparents by phone, and the families all send letters and pictures to each other, but Bill misses having his grandparents around, especially at Thanksgiving and Christmas and at birthday parties. Bill feels jealous of his friends in school who see their grandparents.

After a few months in their new home, Bill's parents joined a church. In October the minister gave a sermon about how hard it was for families to celebrate Thanksgiving when they and their relatives often lived so far apart. He said that in the church there were many older people whose children and grandchildren lived in other parts of the country and many young families who lived far away from their parents and grandparents. He said he hoped to offer grandchildren foster grandparents and grandparents foster grandchildren not only for the holidays but for all year round.

That Thanksgiving Dorothy and Julius Potter came to Bill's house for Thanksgiving dinner. It was love at first sight! Grandpa Julius knew how to play the guitar and said he would teach Bill's sister. Grandma Dorothy belonged to a bowling team and said she'd take Bill along and teach him how to bowl. That was two years ago, and Bill and his family see the Potters very often. Bill still keeps in touch with his New York grandparents. He can't wait for them to visit and meet the Potters. He's sure they will all like each other.

GRANDPARENTS' RIGHTS

Parents have very important rights where their children are concerned, and because this is necessary, lawyers and judges—and some parents themselves—have not thought very much about grandparents' rights until quite recently. One reason for this is that once in a great while grandparents may try to take their grandchildren away from a father or a mother for selfish and wrong reasons. Sometimes this happens because grandparents are too angry to really understand what they are doing; sometimes they really think it is the right thing to do.

Fred's mother was killed in a car accident when his father was driving. His mother's parents were so grief-stricken that they called his father "a murderer" and tried to prove in court that he was an "unfit father." There was a big fight for two years and for a while Fred went to live with his grandparents. He was a very unhappy boy; he'd lost his mother, and now the rest of his family were fighting about him. That's a bad thing to happen to a child.

In another case the grandparents belonged to a religion that had some very strict rules. When Gerald's mother died, they tried to get custody of Gerald because his father had long hair and a beard and drank beer, all things they considered to be sinful.

So, for many years, most of the laws about divorce

and death and child custody left it entirely up to the parent to decide whether or not a child saw his or her grandparents. This has been changing during the last ten or fifteen years, mostly because there are so many more divorces and because so many grandparents have lost touch with their grandchildren.

More than forty states now have special laws saying that grandparents can go to court and ask a judge to give them visitation rights if a parent refuses to let them see a grandchild. Then the judge has to decide what will be "in the best interests of the child." The idea is that while grandparents and parents may have all kinds of complicated feelings about each other, and may even want to hurt each other, a judge will be able to think about the problem more calmly and sensibly.

WHEN THERE ARE MORE THAN FOUR GRANDPARENTS

Debbie's parents were divorced when she was two years old. She still sees all four of the grandparents from that marriage. Then both her father and her mother remarried. Her stepmother has a father and her stepfather has two parents, so suddenly she had seven grandparents. When Debbie was eleven, her mother and her stepfather got a divorce and her mother married another man. This stepfather has a mother and so now Debbie has *eight grandparents*!

As a matter of fact, that is not too unusual these days when so many parents are getting divorced and remarrying. In some ways it can be fun—especially on birthdays and at Christmas time with all those extra presents! It can be pretty upsetting, though, when so many different people all expect you to show you love them. For example, if there is a school play and you're only allowed six tickets, what do you do if you have three parents and five grandparents? Which ones do you invite to the school fair? Which ones do you visit on a school holiday? There are many decisions to be made. Many children feel confused and shy for a long time.

If any of the grandparents blames one of the parents for whatever unhappiness may have caused a divorce, children can feel they are in the middle of a battlefield, which is a most unpleasant feeling. Some parents and grandparents try to get the children to take sides, which is quite unfair. When that happens, it may be a good idea for a child to say, "I want to love all of you; I don't want to have to take sides." If a child feels a little strange when a new set of grandparents appears, it may make things much easier if a child can say, "I need a little time to get used to everything."

Sometimes it can work out very well. Aaron's family includes four grandparents and six stepgrandparents. Fortunately for Aaron, his parents and stepparents have always shown great concern for Aaron and his sister,

Bernice. No matter how the grown-ups may sometimes have felt about each other, every single person in this big family feels that children should never be asked to take sides or get mixed up in any grown-up quarrels. When Aaron recently graduated from high school, all ten grandparents came to the graduation! Aaron's father got special permission from the principal to bring so many people.

After the graduation ceremony, all the grandparents were invited to his first grandmother's house for a party. Aaron said he wanted to make a speech, and he stood up at the table with his glass of punch and said, "I want to thank my parents and my stepparents and my grandparents and my stepgrandparents for loving me and being friends to each other so I could have a happy childhood."

When Amanda's parents got a divorce, Amanda's mother moved two thousand miles away from Amanda's father's mother. This was very hard on Amanda, who was crazy about Grandma Helen. She was afraid she'd never see her again. But Grandma Helen refused to let that happen. She wrote letters and she sent pictures and presents and she called on the telephone. She waited patiently for Amanda's mother to get over being so mad at Amanda's father. She sent a wonderful present when Amanda's mother got married again. She came out to visit when Amanda's mother and stepfather had a baby. Grandma Helen paid for Amanda to go to camp for several summers since her mother and stepfather couldn't afford it. When Amanda was twelve years old, she flew to North Carolina where Grandma Helen lives and stayed two whole months. Sometimes if grandparents can be patient and refuse to be pushed aside—if they keep trying to stay close until feelings cool down—things seem to work out.

Some problems may never be solved, however. People's feelings are just too complicated. If this happens in your family, it's very important to remember this is never, ever, the fault of a grandchild.

The Things You Learn
from Being a Grandchild

MR. Berger's fifth-grade class decided to have a party for grandparents. Mr. Berger suggested that since it was time for him to give an assignment to write a composition, it might be interesting if all the children wrote on the subject, "What I Learn from My Grandparents." On the day of the party each child read his or her composition out loud. Many of the children wrote about such things as learning to ice skate or play cards or how to see the Big Dipper or how to knit or make brownies. But Vivian's composition was about how she learned that every person is different, and Howard wrote about learning how to be generous and kind, and when Pat read her composition about learning how it feels when someone you love dies, everybody got very quiet and some of the grandparents suddenly had to blow their noses and wipe their eyes.

Grandparents can teach many things. Some are very important, and a grandchild may remember them for his or her whole life. Caroline's grandmother, who was a birdwatcher, taught Caroline to recognize hundreds of different birds and gave her field glasses for her tenth birthday. Caroline learned about the way birds live and build nests and migrate. She became so interested in birds that she thought she'd like to become an ornithologist, a person who studies birds, when she grew up. Lottie, an older woman who is a grandmother herself, says, "Every time I look at a beautiful sunset, I remember my grandfather saying 'going, going, gone' as the sun disappeared. It was magic. Now I do the same thing with *my* grandchild."

We learn how to make things and how to do things and how to look and how to listen from grandparents, but even more important, we learn about how people feel and act at different stages of their lives, and about the ways in which young people and older people can show they care about each other.

SENSITIVE FEELINGS

Irene's grandmother gave her a bathrobe for Christmas. Irene thought it was the ugliest thing she had ever seen. When she opened the package on Christmas morning, she gulped and almost choked, but then she said, "Oh, Grandma, it's lovely." She said that because even though she had learned that her grandmother had terrible taste in clothes, she knew her grandmother loved her very much and would be very hurt if Irene showed her disappointment. What Irene had done was to tell a white lie. It's not telling the exact truth, but it is what people do when they don't want to hurt a person's feelings. Often grandparents have different ideas and tastes and opinions, and sometimes you may decide it is better to tell a white lie than to upset them. What we have to figure out for ourselves is just when this is absolutely necessary and not to do it too often. Most of the time—with parents and friends and teachers—telling the truth is a much better idea.

Barry's grandmother often has bad breath. She wears dentures and she also has some trouble with her digestion. When Barry was five years old, he said, "Grammy, your mouth smells." Grandma's feelings were hurt, and tears came to her eyes. Barry learned as he got older that if you love someone you need to think carefully about what you say to them.

Sometimes grandparents visit at a time that is not very convenient. A friend is having a birthday party, or there is an important Little League game in another town, or your parents had promised you could go to one of the movies about outer space that your grandparents wouldn't want to see. It's hard at such times to be polite and to tell a white lie by acting very happy and not upset about your plans being changed.

You can tell your parents when you feel disappointed more easily than you can tell your grandparents. Grandparents' feelings seem to get hurt more easily, maybe because they grew up at a time when children were always expected to be very polite and very loving. But being kind and caring about their feelings is a sort of practice for being caring about other people when you grow up.

Melanie told her mother, "I was so mad when you told me I couldn't go camping because Poppa and Nanny were coming for the weekend, but when I hugged and kissed them and told them how glad I was to see them, it made them so happy that I felt much better."

DIFFERENT WAYS OF LOVING

Grandparents also help us to learn that no two people are ever alike, that you can love many people and that you may need to express that love in many different ways. One grandfather may have a terrific sense of humor and know some very funny jokes, while another grandfather may be very serious. One grandparent may be shocked if you say "damn," while another grand-parent may even say words that shock *you*. One grand-mother may like to stay home and bake cakes and cookies, while another grandmother wants to become a congresswoman. One grandfather may be quiet and patient and love to read to a grandchild, while another grandfather is restless and impatient and likes to keep busy playing tennis or painting the house or mowing the lawn.

Grandparents give us practice in different ways of loving and being loved. Maryann knows that when Grandma Jensen gets off the plane, she can run into her arms and hug her so hard that they almost fall over together. Grandma Jensen hugs her right back and they laugh out loud. When Grandma Grendon comes to visit, Maryann kisses her on the cheek very politely and then stands back so her grandmother can say, "My, how you have grown." Oscar knows that his father's mother will want to hear how he's doing in fourth grade, but his mother's father will ask him about his pitching.

Maryann and Oscar have found out that there are different ways to show love to different kinds of people. That is an important thing to learn, because knowing how to get along with all the different kinds of people there are in the world can help you to have a happy personal life and lead to a peaceful world.

GIVING AND RECEIVING

Nick has five brothers and sisters, all older than he is. Grandma Charlotte was coming to stay for Christmas, and Nick was feeling terrible because he couldn't think of anything he could give his grandmother that would be as good as the things his brothers and sisters could buy for her. He was only seven, so his allowance was too small for any kind of expensive present. But Grandma Charlotte was one of his most favorite people and he wanted to show her how much he loved her.

Nick thought and thought, and finally he wrote Grandma Charlotte a letter and sealed it in an envelope that he put under the Christmas tree. When Grandma opened the letter on Christmas morning, this is what she read:

> *Dear Grandma:*
> *Merry Christmas! My present to you is that I want to be your servant for every day of your visit. I will bring you breakfast in bed every day. And on the day you go home, I will carry all your suitcases to your car.*
> > *I love you,*
> > *Nick*

Grandma was not making it up when she told Nick

that was one of the most wonderful presents she'd ever gotten in her whole life.

Sometimes, when we are very young, it seems as if grandparents should do all the giving. Little children have a hard time controlling those feelings that can make you want more and more and more toys. And grandparents have a hard time saying "no." But as we get older, we find out something very important. Nick felt more excited about making Grandma Charlotte so happy than he did about the presents she gave him for Christmas, even though they were things he had wanted very much. Each day, when he took the breakfast tray into the guest room, he felt so *good*. Making someone else happy is one of the nicest kinds of feelings we can ever have.

Ricky made a clay vase for his grandfather's birthday. He loved making things out of clay, but he wasn't at all satisfied with the way the vase turned out. Inside his head he had a picture of a perfect vase. This one was a little uneven around the edges. When his grandfather made a big fuss about how wonderful the vase was, Ricky got very suspicious. "Grandpa, you're just telling me you think it's a wonderful vase because you love me," Ricky said. His grandfather thought for a minute and then he said, "Ricky, you're absolutely right, and it's the best reason I can think of!"

Most children can't give grandparents fancy, expensive presents like the ones they often get from them. But that certainly doesn't seem to bother most grandparents. They much prefer to receive a gift that shows how much you care. When Barbara copied one of her stories onto colored paper and decorated each page, her grandmother said, "This will be one of my great treasures." What Barbara learned is that her grandmother knew how hard she had worked on her present, and that fact made it more precious to her.

If you want to understand why grandparents seem to like things that you make yourself, you might say to a grandparent, "You're always telling me that you like things I make myself, but you always give me presents you buy in a store. *I* would like to have something *you* made yourself!" Sometimes grandparents forget that maybe grandchildren would feel very good getting something made just for them, too.

Fern has a rag rug that her grandfather made on the floor next to her bed. Every time she puts her bare feet down on the rug, she thinks about her grandfather and how he learned to make rugs after he retired. Philip has a crayon sketch on the wall over his desk. It's a picture of a lighthouse that his grandmother drew on a trip to Cape Cod. It's not a great work of art, but now he knows how good it feels to get a present that tells something very personal about someone you love.

Giving is more than just presents. Holding Grandma's arm when she walks after a hip operation is giving; listening to Grandpa tell you about when he was in the Second World War is giving your time and attention, which can be the most important gift of all.

LEARNING ABOUT GETTING OLD

One thing you need to know about grandparents is that no matter how old they may seem to you, inside their heads they usually still feel young. It might be interesting to ask your grandparents how old they feel inside their heads. When Karen asked her grandma this question, her grandma said, "I still think of myself as the young girl your grandpa married." Nan's grandfather said, "Inside my head I'm thirty-five years old and very handsome!" Thirty-five sounded pretty old to Nan, but her grandfather was sixty-five at the time.

Brian would get very confused when his grandmother said that she was playing bridge "with the girls," or that she was going to a movie "with the girls." Finally he asked his mother if these were "the girls with the Grandma faces." His mother laughed and said that was exactly right.

Most grandparents don't think of themselves as being old. It all happened so gradually. Lisa's grandma told her, "When I look at Pop Pop, I don't even notice his gray hair and his wrinkles. To me he's still the young man in the picture I showed you, when he was a young soldier in the army, before we got married." Even though they think of themselves as young, most grandparents understand that to you they probably seem old. But it can still hurt their feelings if you talk too much about their being very old.

Grandparents can range in age from the late forties to sixty or seventy or even eighty years old. Some grandparents really *are* young. Forty-five or fifty-three may sound very, very old to you, but people who are that age usually don't feel old at all and are likely to be as active and full of energy as your parents are. Because grandparents can be many different ages and because each grandparent has his or her own feelings about getting older, one of the best things you can do is to watch and listen and make up your own mind about what it means to be the oldest generation.

Newborn babies give you good feelings about the beginnings of life. You know about childhood from your own experiences, and you are learning from your parents and other grown-ups about how it feels to be twenty and thirty and forty years old. Grandparents help you to understand the later years of life.

Some grandparents seem very strong and healthy and can do just about anything. Some grandparents are not so well. They may have pains in their fingers and knees from arthritis, or have to live a certain kind of life because of having had a heart attack. Some grandparents don't have any sickness a doctor can find, but they say they feel sick very often. This may be because they are worrying about getting old. You can learn a lot about how different people deal with illness and aging from watching grandparents. Some older people struggle very hard to go on taking care of themselves; others get frightened and want to be taken care of.

One of Emily's grandmothers has cancer. She has a lot of pain, but when she feels very bad, she just wants to be left alone. She says, "I can't stand being pitied!" This grandmother tries hard not to let other people see how she feels. She tries hard to go on working, and when she has to go to the hospital for treatment, she doesn't want anyone to come to see her. Emily's other grandmother says she's very weak and frail, but Emily doesn't understand how this can be so. When this grandmother wants to go away on a trip, she seems fine. But if Emily talks back or does anything her grandmother thinks is impolite, she says, "I'm too sick to be treated this way."

People have different ways of dealing with retirement as well as with health and illness. Russell's grandfather says he could hardly wait for the day he could retire—there were so many marvelous things he wanted to do that he'd never had time for before. Anthony's grandparents both work as volunteers in a hospital. They say they never worked harder in their whole lives and they love it. Anthony's grandfather says, "We spent our lives running a cleaning store, and while there is nothing wrong with cleaning people's clothes, that's *nothing* compared to helping people who are sick and frightened."

Ingrid's grandfather, on the other hand, seems to feel as if his whole life is over. Ingrid heard him talking in the kitchen to her mother. He said, "All my life I've been Arnold, the policeman. Now I'm Arnold, the nothing." When Ingrid heard him say that, she ran into the kitchen and said, "That's not true—you're Arnold, the father and grandfather and friend!" Ingrid's grandfather began to cry and Ingrid was afraid she had done something terrible. Then her grandfather hugged her hard and said, "Sometimes children are smarter than grown-ups."

Some people prepare way ahead of time for the years when they will retire from their jobs. They know just what they will do. Others let retirement creep up on them. They don't want to think about it at all, and when it happens, they get very sad and angry. Some people enjoy life more than they ever did before, while others seem unhappy almost all the time. Some grandparents have more energy than they know what to do with—they are always on the go—while other grandparents talk about feeling old and tired.

Watching all these different kinds of feelings and

behavior can help you to think about the kind of person you hope you will be when you get old. It's a very long way off, but the truth is that if your grandparents had thought about getting older when they were young, they might have been able to prepare themselves much better for this time of their lives.

YOU DIDN'T DO IT

It's important to remember that children are *never* responsible for sad events—like being sick or alone or worrying about money—that may happen to older people. Children are also not responsible for trying to make things get better. That is a problem for grown-ups. There may be many times when you wish you could change what happens and take away the bad things, but you can't, and while you may feel sad about that, there is no need to feel guilty about it. Some problems that can arise in a family—like a serious illness or a death—are just not things a child can do anything about.

But often grandchildren can help grandparents who seem to have problems about getting older. If a grandparent says, "I wish I could do all kinds of things with you, like going on a hike or playing ball," a grandchild may say, "I can do those things with lots of other people, but *you* taught me how to play chess and *you* read me wonderful stories about Robin Hood!"

If a grandparent is sick and in pain, sometimes nothing can make that person feel better than to have a grandchild hold his or her hand. Very often when older people feel frightened or sad or worried about getting old, the one thing in all the world that can make them feel better is to be with a grandchild. You can give them the special kind of love they have given you.

WHEN A GRANDPARENT CHANGES

Paula's grandmother talks funny. She had a stroke, and now when she tries to say something, she can't get the words out. Lenny's grandfather talks to himself. He doesn't even recognize Lenny anymore. Sometimes changes that happen in the brains of older people make them behave in ways that seem very strange. This can be sad and frightening. But if it happens to your grandparent, it's important to remember that even if he or she can't seem to talk to you, or forgets your name, that doesn't mean he or she doesn't love you anymore.

Hilary's grandmother seemed to become more and more confused, and often Hilary couldn't figure out what she was talking about. At first Hilary was frightened; this wasn't the grandmother she had known, who had told her such funny stories. One time when she went to visit her grandmother, it sounded as if her grandmother was talking baby talk. Hilary ran out of the room and cried. What was wrong with her grandmother?

Hilary's father said, "I know how painful this is for you, Hilary. Grandma has a disease called Alzheimer's disease. Nobody can catch it from her. It's caused by changes in the brain. She can't remember things. She gets confused and very frustrated. It's frightening for her to know she is forgetting more all the time. She won't get better. But even though she sounds kind of weird, inside her head she still loves you. If you could just hold her hand for a few minutes and then give her a hug, she would know, inside, that you love her."

Hilary couldn't do it that time, but she thought about it a lot and she went back two weeks later. She sat on a chair next to her grandmother and remembered all the good times they had had together, and she took her grandma's hand. Her grandma's eyes filled with tears, and then Hilary knew that somewhere, deep inside, Grandma still loved her and knew who she was. It was painful, but Hilary went to see her grandmother until things got so bad that Grandma had to go to a nursing home. Hilary's father said, "You said good-by to Grandma all the times you held her hand. You don't have to see her anymore."

Of all the things that are not so wonderful in life,

nothing is harder than to watch someone you love get old and sick and die, and sometimes this can happen between grandchildren and grandparents. There is no way that anyone can take away the pain that a child can feel, but there are things each person can do about sadness and pain. We can learn from it; we can find out more and more about what it means to be a human being. We can find ways to use our suffering to make us better people.

Annette's grandmother is old and sick. She has rheumatoid arthritis, which means she is crippled and has a great deal of pain. Annette can hardly bear seeing her grandmother. She remembers how it was before Granny got sick. She loves her grandmother and can't stand seeing her suffer so much. When Granny cries, Annette runs to the garage and cries, too. But sometimes she can't help herself—she feels angry. She isn't allowed to bring friends home and she has to be quiet all the time. Once or twice she even had a terrible thought—that her life would be better if her grandmother died. Such thoughts make her feel that she's a terrible, mean person.

Annette is none of those things. She's just a human being who is having a very hard and unhappy time. She needs to accept the fact that her mixed feelings are natural and nothing to be ashamed of.

One day Annette's father found her crying in the

garage. He said, "Honey, I know this is a very bad time for all of us. Granny never, never wanted you to suffer on her account, but she can't help herself and we can't stop taking care of her." That night Annette's parents decided that she could go to a sleep-away camp that summer, even though it would be a big expense for them. Her father said, "You need some relief, some time away from all this. You've been a wonderful grandchild and Granny knows it."

Jeremy's grandmother died three months ago. Now his grandfather sits in his room and thinks about his wife and cries. Jeremy feels so upset. He misses his grandmother and he feels sad, too, but he wishes his grandfather hadn't come to live in his house, and he wishes his grandfather would stop crying so much. Jeremy's mother tells him, "You have to be patient. Grandma and Grandpa lived together for forty-five years and loved each other a lot. Grandpa needs time to remember and to grieve." Jeremy understands, but he still feels impatient and upset.

Sometimes a child can help a grandparent begin to feel better after he or she has been sick or widowed. After a while it might be a good idea to suggest going someplace and doing something together. If Jeremy can be a little more patient, the day will come when his grandfather will start to pick up the pieces of his life. If one day Jeremy sees his grandfather is not crying and sitting at the window, he might say, "Grandpa,

I'll bet I know what Grandma would like us to be doing on a beautiful day like today. She'd want us to take a picnic to the park."

It is never a child's fault when a grandparent is sick or unhappy. But sometimes children can help their grandparents feel better if the children find some good way to say, "Hey, there are still interesting things to do, and we love you."

WHEN A GRANDPARENT DIES

Jan once asked her grandmother, "Are you so old you're going to die soon?" At first Grandma was shocked and upset. But when she thought it over, she realized that Jan's question was an important one. She told Jan that she expected to live for a long time, but that she, too, sometimes thought about dying. Jan asked, "Do you feel scared?" Her grandmother answered, "I guess anybody who is getting old gets scared sometimes. I worry about getting sick and needing to have people take care of me. All my life I liked to take care of other people. I worry about being a burden to you and your mommy and daddy. What I try to do is keep busy doing things I like to do and helping other people, so I haven't got too much time to think about it." Jan felt good, because now she knew it would be all right to ask Grandma questions about things that worried her.

Some grandparents don't want to talk about old age

and dying. Ted's grandfather worked so hard all his life that he never had much fun. His wife died before he retired, and now he's all alone. Ted's grandfather feels bitter and angry and lonely. He doesn't want to talk about his life or his age or anything very personal. When Ted asked him a question about Grandma's death, his grandfather went into another room. Ted's father said, "Ted, you'll have to understand that when my father was young, nobody in his family ever talked about feelings. He was taught that big boys never cried or talked about loving somebody. I don't think we can change him now. The best we can do is to let him know we love him by listening to him talk about how hard his life has been. Sometimes, even when you want to help a person, you can't if they won't let you."

Ted asked his father and mother questions about getting old and dying. They answered as carefully and honestly as they could. If some questions upset older people, it's a better idea to ask someone else.

Lori's grandfather had cancer. Nobody tried to keep Lori from knowing about it. When Grandpa died, Lori went to the funeral and cried and hugged her parents and her grandmother. Everybody talked about Grandpa. Lori kept pictures of him on her dresser. At school she made a cookbook of all her grandfather's favorite recipes, which her grandmother wrote out for her, and copies of it were sold at the school fair. Lori felt good knowing so many other people would get to eat the double chocolate cake and lasagna and all the other things her grandfather had loved so much.

Long before Grandpa died, when he had to go to the hospital for an operation, Lori's parents told her he was very sick and probably wouldn't live very long. Lori's mother said, "We want Grandpa to know how much we love him and how we will miss him. We don't want him to feel lonely at this hard time of his life."

Grandma brought Grandpa home when nothing else could be done for him in the hospital. Every time Lori visited her grandfather, he seemed thinner and weaker, and she felt scared and sad. But she went to see him often and she told him all about school and her friends. She would sit on the bed and hold Grandpa's hand. It was thin and trembly, and sometimes she wanted to run away. But Grandpa looked at her with such love in his eyes that she forgot about everything else. One day, when Grandpa was very weak and seemed too tired even to open his eyes, Lori leaned over and said, "Grandpa, I love you so much, and I'll never, ever forget you." She saw two tears run down her grandfather's cheeks, and she held his hand harder than ever.

A few days later Grandpa died. Lori cried and cried. She knew she would miss her grandfather for as long as she lived. But she was so glad there had been those special afternoons with him, and she felt proud of herself because she had been brave enough to say goodby.

Some parents have the mistaken idea that it is possible to protect their children from the sadness of old age and dying. When Ellen was eight years old, her grandfather died very suddenly while she was away at summer camp. She didn't find out about it until she came home, long after the funeral. Her parents and her aunts and uncles didn't want to talk to her about what had happened. Ellen felt lonelier than ever before in her whole life. Whenever one of the grown-ups began to cry, someone would tell Ellen to go and play in her room. She would stare out the window, trying to understand what was happening. She couldn't believe she'd never see her grandfather again. She wanted to cry but she couldn't seem to do it. It wasn't until Ellen was a grown-up woman that she finally was able to cry for her grandfather.

It probably would have been better if Ellen had been brought home from camp so that she could go to her grandfather's funeral. Then she could have shared her sorrow with the people she loved and she would have been able to cry. Crying is an important way of expressing sad feelings. Funerals are the way in which families share their grief. They need each other; they need to feel love all around them. Children who are not allowed to share in the family ceremonies don't feel protected—they just feel shut out.

There are many things in life that are worth feeling sad about. The illness or the death of a grandparent may be the first time that young children have to face what is a natural part of life. It is probably the most difficult experience they have ever had. But children usually feel much better if they can share sad times with the people they love.

WAYS OF REMEMBERING

A grandparent stays with you forever, in your memories, even after he or she dies. Every time Edith passes a bakery, she is reminded of the times she baked cakes and cookies with her grandmother. One day Dominick saw a beautiful lamp in the window of an antique store, and he remembered his grandfather telling him all about Tiffany lamps and how he loved them.

Sometimes things that belonged to that person help us to remember him or her. Seth asked if he could have his grandfather's cane. Cynthia has her grandmother's silk scarves that still smell of her perfume. Eric has his grandfather's collection of pipes and the album of pictures of when his grandfather was a boy. Jerry loves to look at his grandfather's old schoolbooks.

They seem so strange. His grandfather once told him, "It may be hard to learn to read, but at least your books aren't all about Dick and Jane!"

If we try to remember only the good memories about someone who has died, they will fade very quickly. What we need to do is think about all the kinds of memories we may have, so we can hold onto a whole person.

After his grandfather's funeral, Alex felt guilty when he realized that he was thinking about the time his grandfather spanked him. Once when Alex was visiting his grandparents, he got into the car in the driveway and accidentally released the brake. The car began rolling down the hill. His grandfather ran after it, got in and put on the brake. Then he spanked Alex hard because he had been so frightened. Alex asked his father if he was thinking about Grandpa, and if he remembered anything bad. Alex's father said, "I remember the good times and the bad times. I remember when my father made me happy and I remember when he made me angry. Grandpa was a person, a man— he was a human being. If I want to remember him, I have to remember what he was really like."

After Alex's father said that, Alex suddenly remembered the time his grandfather took him on a fishing trip and how excited he got when Alex caught a bigger fish than the men on the boat. He had taken a picture of Alex and his fish. Alex decided he wanted to put that picture on his wall.

Remembering that you felt angry and impatient when your grandparent got old and sick is nothing to be ashamed of. It is normal to be upset about having to be very quiet, and it can be frightening to see someone you love looking awfully sick. It is also quite normal to feel very angry at a grandparent who dies. How could Grandpa *do* such a thing, when you loved him so much? He had no right to leave you. It seems like a foolish and mean feeling, but it is one that everyone has when someone they love dies.

It is possible to have three or four or more different kinds of feelings at the same time, and any feeling a person has is a normal feeling. It's much better to let ourselves feel all our feelings than to try to stop some of them because we think they are crazy or wrong.

What we *do* about our feelings is what is most important. At the beginning of this book, I said that you are your grandparents' future. When a grandparent dies, the most important thing that he or she leaves behind is *you*! Your feelings of sadness will never go away altogether, but you will begin to feel better as time passes, and it will make you feel good to know that because of your memories, you will be able to take your grandparents with you, into your future life.

You Are the Future

YOUR grandparents can tell you about the past, and they can share the present time in your life, but the future—the time when you become a grown-up person—belongs to you. Sometimes grandparents may say that you are *their* future, and it can be pretty confusing.

The reason why grandparents may talk about your being their future is that they know they are the oldest generation in the family. They know they will die someday, and they hope that future generations in the family will remember them. People usually need to feel that they will remain a part of life through the people they love, and grandchildren who will grow up and probably marry and have children of their own represent that special feeling of a family going on and on and on.

Sometimes, when you see a picture of a grandmother or a grandfather when he or she was your age, you may be very startled to realize how much you look like that picture. Sometimes a grandmother will say, "You sure have Grandpa's sense of humor!" Or your mother might say, "You have your grandfather's temper, all right!" That's one of the ways grandparents feel that their lives will go on, in a certain sense, even after they die.

YOUR SPECIAL LIFE

When grandparents think about the future, they want everything to be better than it was during their lifetimes. They want you to be kinder, smarter, happier, more generous, better able to use more of your talents than they ever were. It's a natural feeling on their part, but it can get to be too big a burden for a grandchild.

What you have to decide for yourself is how to think of your grandparents with love and to make them part of your life as you grow up, but not in such a way that you don't live the special life that is right for the special person you are.

Henry's father and grandfather are both excellent plumbers, and they talk about the time when Henry can become the third generation in the plumbing business. Henry is very close to his grandmother and one day Henry told her, "It makes me feel angry when Daddy and Grandpa talk about me becoming a plumber. I want to drive one of those great big trucks that go all over the country!" Grandma said, "Don't worry, Henry. If that's what you still want to do when you grow up, you just be the best truck driver you can be, and Daddy and Grandpa will be proud of you."

The hardest part of being your grandparents' future comes after a grandparent dies. "I feel bad because I never let my grandma teach me how to knit," Claudia said. "Now I'm older and more patient. I want my mother to teach me, because I know it would have made my grandmother happy." Claudia's mother said, "Sure—I'll teach you, and if you enjoy knitting, that will be fine. But if you get bored or impatient, don't worry about it. Your grandma would have understood how you feel."

Being the best you can be at whatever you do is the best way to be your grandparents' future. Jacob made a big mistake. He has had the feeling, from as far back as he can remember, that he would like to be an actor when he grows up. He is always in the school plays, and he usually gets the best parts. He feels happier on a stage or going to the theater than at any other time. But his grandfather made fun of him. He'd say, "Acting is for sissies. What you need to do, Jacob, is work hard at your mathematics. That's where the future lies." Not long before he died, his grandfather said, "I'll pay for you to go to a camp where they teach all about computers. If you want to make a good living when you grow up, you better learn about computers."

Jacob wanted to go to a camp where they gave a lot of plays and where he could learn about set design and theatrical lighting. Instead, he told his parents he would go to a computer camp because that would have pleased his grandfather. That is *not* a good way to remember somebody you love.

Parents and grandparents are sometimes wrong in telling you something very specific they hope you will do. You may need to say to yourself, "I know my grandfather loved me and wanted me to be happy, so I will have to decide what I want to do so that I *can* be happy."

SHARING YOUR FUTURE

Of course, there are special things about grandparents that we want to make a part of our lives forever—good memories that we want to keep in the family. I love to remember my grandfather telling me stories about flowers. I told my daughter the same stories and I will tell them to my granddaughter. I will also tell her stories about how her great-grandfather came to America from Russia when he was six years old and how he felt when he saw the Statue of Liberty and met his older brothers and sisters at Ellis Island. I'll tell her because I loved to hear that story when I was a little girl, and it is part of our family history.

I have a little china bird with a big open mouth. My grandfather used to put a fifty-cent piece in the bird's mouth once a week, for me. Someday I'll give that china bird to my granddaughter. It's a family antique with a story. I know her grandfather will tell her lots of wonderful stories that his father told him when he was a child and that he told his own daughter.

But there is one thing I know we will *never* tell our granddaughter, and that is that she should do the same things that we did. She is surely our future, but our dream about the future is that she will be a person who will find out what she needs to do and be in order to feel good about herself.

There are many ways to take your grandparents with you, in your thoughts and memories, as you grow up. The good ways to do this are those that make you feel good about what you are doing.

When his grandfather died, Danny decided to give part of his allowance to the soup kitchen in his grandfather's church because his grandfather had worked as a volunteer there and had been very concerned about people who were out of work and hungry. He wanted his grandfather's work to go on.

Betty started a paper route when her grandfather died. She wanted to make enough money so she could take guitar lessons, because her grandfather had left her his guitar. It was something she felt she would enjoy a lot.

Neil's and Herbie's grandmother took them on a trip to Israel the summer after their grandfather died. She said, "Grandpa always wanted to visit Israel, but then he got sick and we never could go. It would have made him so happy to know you are seeing all the things he wanted to see." During their visit to Israel, Grandma had a birthday. Neil and Herbie found out from a cousin who lived in Israel how they could buy a tree and plant it in one of the orchards. On the birthday card they gave their grandmother, they wrote, "This is so we can remember that Grandpa was part of this trip and something from him will stay here after we go home."

Doing things that make you feel full of love, doing things that are comforting, doing things that keep happy memories alive—these are the ways to bring your grandparents with you into your future. And most of all, growing up to be a person who likes to be who he or she is—becoming more and more your own special self—is the best way to share your future with someone you loved who loved you.

When my mother died, we planted a tree in her

memory in the front yard of our house. Now my daughter and my son-in-law and my granddaughter live in that house, and the tree has grown very tall and beautiful. Every time I see it, I think that pretty soon my granddaughter will be old enough to climb that tree, and it makes me feel as if her great-grandmother's arms will be around her as she climbs through the branches.

I would like her always to feel that she is surrounded by the loving arms of all the people in her family, and I will surely tell her how much her great-grandmother would have loved her. But when she gets to the top of the tree and can look in all directions and see what the world looks like, she'll be able to pick out the places *she* wants to go and the things *she* wants to do. The tree of memory will always be there, but it will only be the beginning of her future.